My Big Gay
Italian Funeral

Anthony J. Wilkinson

A Samuel French Acting Edition

FOUNDED 1830

SAMUELFRENCH.COM
SAMUELFRENCH-LONDON.CO.UK

FOR PRODUCTION ENQUIRIES

UNITED STATES AND CANADA
Info@SamuelFrench.com
1-866-598-8449

UNITED KINGDOM AND EUROPE
Plays@SamuelFrench-London.co.uk
020-7255-4302

Each title is subject to availability from Samuel French, depending upon
country of performance. Please be aware that *MY BIG GAY ITALIAN
FUNERAL* may not be licensed by Samuel French in your territory.
Professional and amateur producers should contact the nearest Samuel
French office or licensing partner to verify availability.

No one shall make any changes in this title(s) for the purpose of production. No part of this book may be reproduced, stored in a retrieval system, or transmitted in any form, by any means, now known or yet to be invented, including mechanical, electronic, photocopying, recording, videotaping, or otherwise, without the prior written permission of the publisher. No one shall upload this title(s), or part of this title(s), to any social media websites.

For all enquiries regarding motion picture, television, and other media rights, please contact Samuel French.

MUSIC USE NOTE

Licensees are solely responsible for obtaining formal written permission from copyright owners to use copyrighted music in the performance of this play and are strongly cautioned to do so. If no such permission is obtained by the licensee, then the licensee must use only original music that the licensee owns and controls. Licensees are solely responsible and liable for all music clearances and shall indemnify the copyright owners of the play(s) and their licensing agent, Samuel French, against any costs, expenses, losses and liabilities arising from the use of music by licensees. Please contact the appropriate music licensing authority in your territory for the rights to any incidental music.

IMPORTANT BILLING AND CREDIT REQUIREMENTS

If you have obtained performance rights to this title, please refer to your licensing agreement for important billing and credit requirements.

MY BIG GAY ITALIAN FUNERAL was first produced by Bianco Productions in New York City Off-Broadway at St. Luke's Theatre. The play had its first preview on June 1st, 2013 and opened on June 16, 2013. The production was directed by Sonia Blangiardo and general managed by 22Q Entertainment with costume design by Emily DeSimone. The Production Stage Managers were Robert Levinstein and Sandra Trullinger. The cast was as follows:

MAURIZIO	Brett Douglas
ANTHONY	Anthony J. Wilkinson
ONDINE	Beth Dzuricky
ANGELA	Donna Castellano
MARIA	Marissa Perry
TONIANN	Debra Toscano
PETER	Brian Patrick Murphy
LUCIA	Liz Gerecitano
DOMINICK	Mustafa Gatollari
CONNIE/EVA/AUNT DONNA	Meagan Robar
RABBI HOWIE HOROWITZ/LOU/DRAG QUEEN #1	Chad Kessler
VIDAL/DRAG QUEEN #2	Erik Ransom
EZIO	Brandon Goins
FEMALE SWING	Marie Fontaine

CHARACTERS

ANTHONY PINNUNZIATO – Male, 30s. Our everyman. Stereotypical Italian-American boy next door type. Lead.

PETER PINNUNZIATO – Male, 30s. Anthony's slightly younger brother whom he despises. Lead.

MAURIZIO LEGRANDE – Male, 30 to 50. Any ethnicity. Outlandishly dressed, over-the-top, flamboyant. Has an accent that cannot be pegged down. Lead.

ANGELA PINNUNZIATO – Female, late 40s - 60. Lovingly overbearing, overpowering mother hen. Rules the roost with an iron fist and a wooden spatula. Anthony's mother. Lead.

MARIA PINNUNZIATO – Female, late 20s to late 30s. Anthony's flighty, sweet and self absorbed baby sister. Aspirations of stardom, but fizzled sense of reality. Hysterical and fancies herself as a Broadway star.

LUCIA FUCCIO – Female, late 20s to late 30s. Brassy and trendy. Anthony's dependable and reliable best friend. A feminine, pretty "lipstick lesbian." Supporting.

DOMINICK VITALE – Male, 30s. The strikingly handsome and suave boyfriend of Peter Pinnunziato. Supporting.

AUNT TONIANN – Female. late 30s to late 40s. Angela's fussy younger sister. Hated her brother-in-law but is there to support and instigate matters. Comedic Actress. Supporting.

ONDINE OZZUPACCI – Female, late 30s to late 50s. Professional martyr and Over-The-Top Crier who crashes the wake and never leaves. Comic relief, great scene stealer. Comedic Actress. Supporting.

CONNIE/EVA/AUNT DONNA – Female, late 20s to early 40s. Comedic sketch actress who can pull off three roles. Connie, another lipstick lesbian with the mouth of a truck driver. Eva, an asian woman who speaks broken English and yells in Chinese. Aunt Donna, Joseph's sister who walks with a cane and is a stereotypical Italian relative who has to be in more pain than anyone else. Supporting.

RABBI HOWIE HOROWITZ/LOU DONATACCI – Male, late 30s to late 40s. Comedic sketch actor who can pull off a Staten Island Guido as well as a very profound Rabbi. Supporting.

DRAG QUEEN/VIDAL – Drag Queen lip syncs at the night club (a disco flashback scene) and transitions the story. Vidal is an over-the-top medium that Maurizio brings in. Supporting.

EZIO – Male, 30s. Strikingly Handsome. Preferably shirtless at the night club as the hot bartender and then resurfaces at the end as the owner of the Funeral Home. Supporting.

SETTING

A funeral home and a night club

TIME

Contemporary

I dedicate this show to the man who inspired me my whole life by demonstrating to perfection what a real parent should be. His influence and contributions to the community were admired by all, and helped change the opinions of so many who surrounded him. He encouraged me to make others laugh and keep others strong by doing so. Dad, this one is for you!

– Anthony J. Wilkinson

ACT ONE

SCENE I – FUNERAL HOME

*(Lights up on an empty funeral parlor. The chairs are lined up in traditional fashion facing the coffin. Flower arrangements are perfectly placed around as we are clearly set for the first viewing of Joseph Pinnunziato. [Directors choice: The coffin can be the fourth wall if a prop coffin is not available] There is a moment of silence at first, then we hear **MAURIZIO** offstage.)*

MAURIZIO. *(offstage)* What do you mean you don't know who I am? This is Staten Island not Siberia. Everyone knows who I am!

*(**MAURIZIO** enters.)*

I'm Maurizio LeGrande of the Palm Beach and Mineola LeGrande's. And Ecto, Endo or whatever your name is, your services will no longer be needed because it was Joe Pinnunziato's dying wish that I take over the direction of his funeral. Therefore any and all questions, visitors, and all phone calls go directly to me.

EZIO. *(offstage)* Suit yourself.

*(**MAURIZIO** makes his way around the funeral home in disgust.)*

MAURIZIO. I wish I had time to decorate this tragic scene of a living room. I will never understand why these crazy Italians love all these pictures and flowers and...

(He stops when he sees Joe in the coffin.)

MAURIZIO. *(cont.)* Well hello there Mr. Pinnunziato. I cleared my schedule just for you. Hard to say no to a dead person. So sorry to hear of your demise. I will do what I can to make sure everything goes smoothly.

(He starts to walk away. Then turns back.)

MAURIZIO. Did you have work done? You look fabulous!

*(**MAURIZIO**'s phone rings. He answers.)*

Hello! This is Maurizio LeGrande how can I help you... Yes...yes I am coordinating all of the services for the deceased. No, we don't need any more flowers...well I don't care who sent them, there are too many here so send them to another dead person.

*(**MAURIZIO** hangs up.)*

EZIO. *(offstage)* Maurizio, we got some more flowers and some nice fruit baskets.

MAURIZIO. Fruit baskets too!?? What is wrong with all of the crazy people on this island! This is a funeral home not the Garden of Eden. Do not bring one more thing in this room!

*(**MAURIZIO** exits. A moment later **ANTHONY** enters the funeral home. Perfectly dressed in a black suit and tie, **ANTHONY** approaches his fathers coffin. Immediately he is struck by the image we don't see and he takes a second to absorb the impact of the fatality of his father. He collects himself then kneels at the coffin.)*

ANTHONY. Daddy...I always knew this day would come, but I guess as much as you prepare yourself for it, you're never quite ready. Even though you were so sick, I just felt so much comfort knowing you were still here... but now you're at peace and that's where you deserve to be. You were always so supportive of me and all my decisions...I just wanted to make you proud. I know I need to stand up now and be a man and take care of the family. You know the next three days are gonna be hell! And for some strange reason I have a feeling you're going be sitting somewhere in this room having a glass of wine taking it all in.

(A voice is heard offstage in hysteria.)

MAURIZIO. *(offstage)* I told you ectoplasm or whatever your stupid name is…the second he arrives you were to let me know. Idiots!! So hard to find good help these days.

(MAURIZIO enters.)

Anthony my dear, how are you?

(They embrace.)

ANTHONY. I'm okay, Maurizio. Thank you so much for doing this.

MAURIZIO. Are you kidding! The second I got the phone call I said clear my schedule. I was supposed to spend the weekend in the Hamptons with Anderson Cooper but of course I canceled under the dreadful circumstances.

ANTHONY. I so appreciate this, you have no idea. This is just going to be one of those awful times and I need all the help I can get.

MAURIZIO. Well that's why I'm here. I must say your father looks incredible.

ANTHONY. Oh please don't say that.

MAURIZIO. But he does, Anthony…

ANTHONY. I mean, it's just…I'm sorry. That always drives me crazy when people come into these wakes and they talk about how good the dead person looks, I mean come on look at him! He's dead! In a box! How good can he look!?

MAURIZIO. You're right, you know, I think some people just don't know what to say and they try to make you feel better.

ANTHONY. If they want to make me feel better they can bring me a shot of tequila. God knows I'm gonna need it by the time this is over.

MAURIZIO. Well I will make sure that we have plenty on standby. Where is Andrew Polinscopy?

ANTHONY. It's Polinsky...and he's stuck in China. He won't be back till after the funeral.

MAURIZIO. I'm sorry to hear that, I will miss him. So your sister is married now?

ANTHONY. No, she's single.

MAURIZIO. Hmm...I'm so confused. The funeral home got a phone call from some random person today named "Peter" who wanted all kinds of information on what was going on and said he wanted to be involved on all the decisions. He said he was the son, but I told them that I did your wedding and I distinctly remember Anthony had a crazy sister, but there was no brother!

ANTHONY. That's correct Maurizio, I don't have a brother.

MAURIZIO. People are so crazy here on this Island of Staten! Who is this Peter person?

ANTHONY. Peter...is my mother's son.

MAURIZIO. Ohhhhh...huh?

ANTHONY. Yes, you see I had a brother but many years ago he stabbed me in the back like he was my worst enemy. So you see now, he's not my brother...he's my Mother's son.

MAURIZIO. Ahhh...of course. You know Anthony, when my brother found out I was gay he didn't like it either. It took him a long time to accept me....

ANTHONY. Oh it has nothing to do with being gay...Peter is gay too!

MAURIZIO. He is? So what happened?! You two should be like gay peas and carrots!

ANTHONY. Please, it's a long story. I don't want to talk about it right now...it's just too much; all of this and knowing he's going to be here. Listen, I don't care who he calls or what he says, I'm the oldest and my father left me in charge. If he has any questions or problems he can come talk to me, and if he knows what's good for him, he won't.

MAURIZIO. I completely understand. Speaking of which, you said you wanted to see the mass cards we picked out. There were so many photos of Saint Anthony I wasn't sure which one you wanted to pick.

ANTHONY. Saint Anthony was my father's favorite Saint.

MAURIZIO. Of course, If you follow me I can take you to see the choices we picked out.

ANTHONY. I can go myself, please stay here. My mother is going to be here any minute and I want to make sure you're here when she arrives. You remember Angela right?

MAURIZIO. Of course, how can I forget!

*(**ANTHONY** exits.)*

Coo-coo family. What did I get myself into again with these crazy Italian people?!

*(**MAURIZIO** goes to fix some flowers just as a woman in black with a veil covering her face begins to enter the room. **MAURIZIO** assumes this is **ANGELA** and pauses, giving her a moment. She slowly begins to enter the room and then in a moment of hysteria she let's out an incredibly large scream and heads for the kneeler.)*

ONDINE. Nooooooooo…

(She drops her head on the kneeler screaming hysterically. She can barely control herself.)

MAURIZIO. I know how hard this must be for you…

ONDINE. Oh you have no idea! He looks so good.

MAURIZIO. I know, I said that too.

ONDINE. They did a nice job.

MAURIZIO. He was a good man.

ONDINE. He was a saint!

MAURIZIO. A good father.

ONDINE. An excellent father!

MAURIZIO. And a good husband to you I am sure.

ONDINE. He's not my husband.

(**MAURIZIO** *pulls up the veil.*)

MAURIZIO. Who are you?

ONDINE. I'm Ondine Ozzupacci, I'm President of the Tuesday Morning Ladies Coffee Clutch. Joe owns the Bowling Alley on Hylan Boulevard, and I have been bowling there for twenty years!

MAURIZIO. Oh, so you are a friend of the family or a mistress?

ONDINE. Oh my God, never a mistress and so much more than a friend, are you kidding? You know how close I am to this family? When I got the call, I almost passed out. I've been hysterical for two days. I feel so terrible. Am I the first one here?

MAURIZIO. You're actually a half hour early…

(**ANTHONY** *re-enters.* **ONDINE** *runs over and grabs him for dear life.*)

ONDINE. Oh Anthony! How could this happen? You must be devastated! How is your sister?

ANTHONY. Holding up.

ONDINE. And Your mother, I can't even imagine.

ANTHONY. Holding her own. I'm sorry, what's your name again?

ONDINE. Ondine. Ondine Ozzupacci from the Tuesday Ladies. Your father every morning when he would see me would look right at me with his tea and say, "Shoot 'em up Ondine!" Oh my God, I can't talk about it. I need to sit.

ANTHONY. Yes, please sit down.

MAURIZIO. Miss, the visiting hours don't start till two.

ONDINE. Am I early?

MAURIZIO. Very. If you wouldn't mind, the immediate family hasn'teven…

ANTHONY. Maurizio, it's fine.

ONDINE. Your mother is gonna want me here Anthony… trust me! Is she on her way?

ANTHONY. I believe so.

ONDINE. Excuse me, Maurizio is it…what time are the services?

MAURIZIO. Two to four and seven to nine, today and tomorrow and the funeral is Wednesday.

ONDINE. Thank you. I'm gonna call work right now and tell them I need off for the next few days so I can be here for the family. Excuse me.

(ONDINE walks upstage and pulls out her phone to call her office.)

MAURIZIO. Did you find a Saint Anthony mass card you like?

ANTHONY. Yes! Thank you! All set.

(ANGELA approaches the entrance with MARIA. MARIA is holding ANGELA who is still in shock. MARIA is bringing her slowly towards the coffin. ANTHONY and MAURIZIO make room for her to come in. ANGELA finally kisses MARIA's forehead and leaves her side and kneels to her husband. Everyone gives her a moment alone as she takes it all in. Then just as ANTHONY is about to approach his Mother, ONDINE swoops in and sits next to her on the kneeler.)

ONDINE. I know, Angela. I know. Just let it out.

ANGELA. As much as you prepare yourself, you're never ready for this ya know.

ONDINE. Trust me! I know! You are NEVER ready. No one knows what you are going through better than me.

ANGELA. I know.

ONDINE. He looks so good though, right?

ANGELA. Peaceful.

(ANTHONY cringes and comes over.)

ANTHONY. Mom, do you want some time alone?

ANGELA. No, I'm okay honey. I'm good.

ONDINE. Angela, I couldn't even believe it yesterday when I got the phone call. I was sitting down having my coffee and the phone rings. Of course I'm thinking it must be my daughter 'cause who else calls me so early, but it wasn't her, it was Angie Cuco! And you know Angie, she never calls unless it's important, so I immediately sit down. Well, when she told me it was Joe Pinnunziato I dropped the phone and lost it. I haven't stopped crying.

ANGELA. I'm sorry, what's your name again?

ONDINE. Ondine! Ondine Ozzupacci from Tuesday Ladies.

ANGELA. Oh yes.

(**MAURIZIO** *now comes over.*)

MAURIZIO. Why don't we let you sit down Miss Ondine so the family can have some time.

ONDINE. That poor woman is in shock.

(**MAURIZIO** *puts* **ONDINE** *in a chair.*)

MARIA. Mommy left me in charge of calling everyone but I never got a chance.

ANTHONY. Oh my God, my phone hasn't stopped. I'm sure on this island everyone knows by now.

ONDINE. Do you need me to make phone calls?

MAURIZIO. I can have someone make phone calls if you need.

ONDINE. Nonsense. I know everyone in your mother's phone. Give me the phone Maria, I'll call everyone and give them the arrangements. God forbid someone didn't see the advance or is out of town, don't panic I'll be right back!

(**ONDINE** *takes the phone and exits.*)

MAURIZIO. Anthony, do you want me to throw this crazy woman out?

ANTHONY. She's harmless. Let her make phone calls; it will keep her busy for a while.

MARIA. Anthony, Peter was at the house this morning.

ANTHONY. And?

MARIA. Listen, he's very anxious about seeing you today.

(**ANGELA** *comes over.*)

ANGELA. I'm gonna tell you right now. I know you two haven't spoken in years and I have stayed silent for a long time. But your father loved both of you! There is nothing that bothered your father more than knowing his two sons could not be in the same room.

ANTHONY. Don't put this on me.

ANGELA. I will put this on you, I'll put it on the two of you! The next few days are gonna be hell. A million people are going to show up to pay respects to your father and I need both my sons with me right now.

ANTHONY. I'm glad he's here for you now. Did you ask him where he was for the last four years when Daddy was sick? Miami's not that far!

ANGELA. He called your father every day! Listen to me Anthony, your father's dying wish was for his two sons to make peace.

ANTHONY. Daddy never said that! I was with him when he died and his last words to me were to make sure I get the money that Gary Gavone owes him.

ANGELA. Those were his last words to you maybe. Maria, what did your father not want more than anything to happen at his funeral?

MARIA. He did say that he wanted Anthony and Peter to make peace for the sake of the rest of the family.

ANTHONY. Look, you don't think I've thought about the fact that Satan's spawn is going to be with me for three days, of course I thought about it! As long as he leaves his miserable excuse for a boyfriend home, we will be fine.

ANGELA. Dominick is his partner! Of course he's going to be here!

ANTHONY. What!? How could you allow that?

ANGELA. Your father liked Dominick!

ANTHONY. Daddy hated Dominick! Dominick is half the reason this family has been broken up for all these years.

MARIA. Dominick has been very nice to me.

ANTHONY. What did he do for you?

MARIA. He got me Lady Gaga tickets for Christmas.

ANTHONY. Oh please! Maurizio, please make sure that when my mother's son Peter arrives, he comes alone. Dominick Vitale is not welcome here.

ANGELA. Anthony Joseph Pinnunziato! You watch your mouth and remember why you are here. This is not about YOU! You're the oldest and I expect you to be the better person and just for now, please for the love of God let it go!

*(**ANTHONY** takes a sigh of frustration and crosses away. **TONIANN** enters making the only loud entrance.)*

TONIANN. Angela, I'm here. So sorry I'm late, the fucking traffic on the island.

ANGELA. Toniann please.

TONIANN. Oh my God Maurizio! How gorgeous you look. You never age.

MAURIZIO. I always liked you.

(They air kiss. She looks towards the coffin.)

TONIANN. Oh my God is that him in there?

ANGELA. No Toniann, it's Elvis. Of course it's him!

(She walks over and kneels trying to get herself to cry. She has an odd moment of not knowing what to feel.)

MARIA. You never loved my father, did you Aunt Toniann?

TONIANN. That's not true, Maria. I loved your father, I just didn't like him. There is a difference. No matter what happened between us, he was still family. It's times like this we all have to stay together. *(She looks at him in the coffin)* He looks so good Angela, they did a nice job.

ANTHONY. Ugh! I hate that! He does not look good. He looks dead! Why do people keep saying that, it makes me crazy!

TONIANN. Anthony, I know how hard this is for you. Listen to me, a lot of people are going to be here. Just stay strong and remember your father loved you very much.

ANTHONY. Thank you!

(*TONIANN goes over to* **MARIA**)

TONIANN. Where is Peter?

MARIA. On his way.

TONIANN. Has he seen Anthony yet?

MARIA. Nope.

TONIANN. Oh shit.

(**ONDINE** *comes flying in with the phone.*)

ONDINE. Everyone is called, Angela! Oh my God Toniann! I am so so sorry.

(**ONDINE** *grabs her into a hug.* **TONIANN** *plays her "emotional" state.*)

TONIANN. Thank you!

ONDINE. How are you holding up?

TONIANN. Barely.

ONDINE. Please, Angie Cuco called me yesterday, I almost passed out when I got the call. I was having my coffee nice like I always do…

(*They drift off upstage in continued conversation.* **TONIANN** *looks to* **ANGELA** *and mouths "who the hell is this?"*)

ANGELA. Maria, call Peter and see if he's lost.

MARIA. I gave him directions before we left.

ANTHONY. Why didn't he just come with you?

ANGELA. He had to stop at The Staaten to make arrangements for the repass.

ANTHONY. What!? I already made arrangements for the repass! Maurizio!

MAURIZIO. Yes, the repass has been arranged at Angelina's. As per your request.

ANGELA. I didn't know you handled that.

ANTHONY. Why the hell would you get him involved?

ANGELA. He needed to do something Anthony! My God it was his father too.

ANTHONY. You're right, we can put him in charge of the guest book. Maurizio, please call and cancel The Staaten.

ANGELA. No Maurizio, don't do that.

ANTHONY. Ma! We're gonna have two repasses now!?

ANGELA. When your brother gets here you two boys, excuse me, you two MEN can discuss it together.

*(**PETER** arrives at the door. Everyone looks to the entrance. **ONDINE** and **TONIANN** take it in and start to cry for him. **ANTHONY** moves towards **MAURIZIO**. **MARIA** and **ANGELA** motion for him, allowing him to come forward and kneel to his Father. He sits and takes it in. He starts to have a moment, but just as he starts to lose it, **ONDINE** and **TONIANN** flock him on opposite sides.)*

TONIANN. I know, sweetie. Let it out.

ONDINE. Terrible.

TONIANN. Your father loved you very much Peter.

ONDINE. He talked about you all the time.

TONIANN. He was so proud of you.

ONDINE. You look just like him.

PETER. He looks...so good.

*(**MAURIZIO** covers **ANTHONY**'s mouth who could clearly explode at this point.)*

ONDINE. He's at peace Peter.

*(**PETER** rises, and hugs his mother and his sister, and takes in a beautiful flower arrangement.)*

PETER. How beautiful the flowers are. They did a nice job.

(He reads a card on the bleeding heart arrangement.)

PETER. "Beloved Father, forever and always, Anthony and Maria."

*(Everyone slowly shoots **ANTHONY** a look. There is a moment of awkward silence. Finally **ANTHONY** takes the pen from the guest book and slowly walks over to the card. He clears his throat and then writes on the card "and P." He crosses back and puts the pen back on the stand. **PETER** goes to read.)*

PETER. "And P"

ANGELA. Anthony!

ANTHONY. There was no room left on the card!

*(**MAURIZIO** enters with a stack of mass cards on a traditional wooden tray.)*

MAURIZIO. Here are the mass cards that you picked out Anthony. They came lovely as you can see.

ANTHONY. Thank you, Maurizio.

*(**PETER** takes a mass card.)*

PETER. Saint Anthony, how appropriate.

ANTHONY. Well Saint Anthony was Daddy's favorite saint.

PETER. Actually, Saint Peter was Daddy's favorite saint. He named ME after Saint Peter.

ANTHONY. Saint Anthony was Daddy's favorite saint, he named ME Anthony.

PETER. He prayed to Saint Peter.

ANTHONY. Well I came first so I guess he liked Saint Anthony more than he liked Saint Peter.

PETER. You were named after Uncle Tony.

ANTHONY. You were named after Peter Cipriani the loan shark that lent Daddy money to buy the bowling alley. He didn't have the vig to pay him one month so he named YOU Peter to keep him happy!

ANGELA. Enough!!! Boys! This is outrageous. If you two want to hate each other for the rest of your lives FINE! I give up! But do not disrespect your father at a time like this. Please!

(The boys go to separate corners. **LUCIA** *enters. She comes in gracefully, passing* **PETER** *first. She knows who he is so she extends her condolences quickly and then goes over to* **ANTHONY** *immediately.)*

ANTHONY. Lucia, thank God you're here.

LUCIA. This must be a nightmare for you.

ANTHONY. You have no idea.

LUCIA. Have you two made up?

ANTHONY. Made up? I'm five minutes into this and I'm ready to kill him!

LUCIA. Anthony, you have to let it go! This isn't the time or the place to bring up the past.

ANTHONY. I know, Lucia. I'm trying, I really am.

LUCIA. Is Dominick here?

ANTHONY. No, But he's coming.

LUCIA. Shut…up!

(Go over to **PETER** *and* **MARIA** *in the other corner speaking quietly)*

PETER. Where is Dominick? I can't do this by myself. It's too much to handle.

MARIA. Calm down Peter, we are all here.

PETER. Oh please, in another ten minutes Anthony's whole posse is gonna show up and as usual…Peter is the bad guy.

MARIA. Whatever happened was a long time ago. No one is going to hold you hostage for something that is so old.

*(An Italian guy [***LOU***] enters the room in sunglasses.* **ANGELA** *turns to* **TONIANN**.*)*

ANGELA. Oh my God. Of all people to show up!

TONIANN. It's the guilt! That son of a bitch.

(**LOU** *comes right over to* **PETER** *and* **ANTHONY** *who move towards him in the coffin area.*)

LOU. Your father was a good man.

ANTHONY. Thank you.

LOU. You don't remember me, do you?

PETER. I don't...

LOU. You boys were young, Maria was just a baby. Lou Donatacci.

ANTHONY. Oh, Lou!

PETER. Thank you so much for coming Lou. If you can make the funeral on Wednesday, we are having a re-pass at the Staaten.

LOU. I'll be there.

(**LOU** *kisses* **PETER**'*s forehead and goes over to* **ANGELA** *to kiss her, but she turns her cheek and is barely cordial.*)

So sorry for your loss, Angela. When your friend called me just now and said you needed me, I was on Hylan and said let me stop in and pay my respects.

TONIANN. We're all good, Lou. Thanks for coming.

LOU. Alright, if you need anything just call me okay.

(**LOU** *exits.*)

ANGELA. If I need anything call him! Is he fucking kidding me? He would be the last person I call!

TONIANN. What fucking nerve! Who the hell called him and said you needed him here?

ONDINE. Oh My God! Was he in your phone?

ANGELA. You called everyone in my phone?

ONDINE. It's times likes this we all have to come together Angela.

ANGELA. He screwed my husband out of so much money years ago when they went partners. If Joey could move he would of lunged for his throat.

ANTHONY. And genius over here invited him to the repass!

PETER. How the hell was I supposed to know!?

ANTHONY. Peter, the second he said Lou Donatacci, you didn't remember who that was?

ANGELA. He wouldn't remember, Anthony.

MARIA. I didn't remember, Anthony.

ONDINE. I'm sure there will be plenty of food.

TONIANN. Oh please! At The Staaten you can fill up on the antipasto alone!

ANTHONY. Maurizio, can you please cancel this repass at the Staaten. Everything is already being taken care of at Angelina's.

PETER. Angelina's!? Maurizio, hold on, we need to talk about this.

ANTHONY. There is nothing to talk about.

PETER. Daddy loved The Staaten!

ANTHONY. Daddy couldn't stand the Staaten. Maurizio, please cancel.

PETER. Maurizio, don't! Daddy was friends with the owner.

ANTHONY. Who died five years ago. A Chinese guy bought the place, you didn't get the memo in Miami?

TONIANN. The Chinese are good luck, Anthony. Peter may be right.

ANTHONY. Lucia, could you back me up on this!

LUCIA. I was with Anthony when he went to Angelina's and she said she would do the right thing and make it comfortable for everyone. She really did.

TONIANN. You gotta admit Angela, she does a nice eggplant.

ONDINE. Her vodka sauce is to die for.

PETER. Fine! Go to Angelina's. I don't even know why I'm here. Anthony has everything under control, right Maurizio?

MAURIZIO. I don't get involved with the family drama.

(DOMINICK enters. ANTHONY takes a moment and makes eye contact then crosses over to a corner and LUCIA immediately joins him. DOMINICK makes his way over to the family. MAURIZIO joins LUCIA and ANTHONY.)

LUCIA. Anthony, calm down.

ANTHONY. This is too much! I don't think I could do this for three days.

MAURIZIO. I'm guessing that is the boyfriend you don't like.

ANTHONY. It's going to take everything inside me not to rip his lungs out. The nerve of him to show up here after what he did.

MARIA. Anthony, stop! You have to think of Daddy now!

LUCIA. It was a long time ago, Anthony, and he is with your brother. Just calm down.

(PETER brings DOMINICK to the coffin.)

DOMINICK. I always said you look just like your Dad.

PETER. He was my best friend.

(ANTHONY cringes but contains himself.)

DOMINICK. He looks so good.

(MAURIZIO and LUCIA cover ANTHONY's mouth again. DOMINICK gets up from the kneeler and walks towards ANTHONY, LUCIA and MAURIZIO.)

MAURIZIO. Maurizio Le Grande of the Palm Beach and Mineola Le Grandes.

DOMINICK. Dominick Vitale. Bensonhurst.

MAURIZIO. Thank you for attending this afternoon. Lovely weather we are having, yes.

DOMINICK. Hey Lucia, long time no see. How are you?

LUCIA. Good, Dominick, good to see you.

(DOMINICK goes over to ANTHONY who has made his way to an isolated corner)

DOMINICK. Anthony, look, I know I'm probably the last person you want to see, but I want you to know that regardless of the past, I am genuinely so sorry for your loss and hope that you can find a way to let it all go and know that Peter is just as upset as you are right now.

ANTHONY. Thanks to you my whole family has been upside down for over a decade and you want to stand here and tell me I need to let it all go. I will never forgive you or my brother for what you did. Don't talk to me. Don't look at me.

*(**ANTHONY** exits. **PETER** comes over.)*

PETER. How did that go?

DOMINICK. Maybe I should leave.

PETER. What!? No. I need you here! Anthony needs to grow up and get over it. You didn't kill anybody.

*(**ONDINE** has now moved to the front row. **CONNIE** enters.)*

TONIANN. Oh Connie!

CONNIE. Toniann! I am so sorry, how you holding up?

TONIANN. Barely. It's all too much.

ANGELA. Thank you for coming, Connie.

CONNIE. I am so so sorry, Angela.

ONDINE. Connie! How are you?

CONNIE. I'm okay, so sorry for your loss.

ONDINE. Thank you.

CONNIE. We must have met at the wedding. Are you Anthony's Aunt?

ONDINE. No. Ondine Ozzupacci from the bowling alley. I remember you when you used to work at Pizza Town years ago.

CONNIE. Oh my God! Yes! How are you?

ONDINE. I've been better. Angie Cuco called me yesterday with the news and I haven't been able to breathe right since I heard.

CONNIE. I'm sure. Let me know if you need any thing.

ONDINE. Thank you.

*(***CONNIE*** *goes over to* **LUCIA** *who is near* **PETER** *and* **DOMINICK**.*)*

CONNIE. Lucia.

LUCIA. Connie.

CONNIE. Had to be the first one here.

LUCIA. Well considering I've been with Anthony attached to his side for the last two weeks, yes.

CONNIE. Really? Funny. Considering I was the first person he called. I was at his house the night it happened. I didn't see you.

LUCIA. That's because I drove his mother to the funeral home.

MAURIZIO. Ladies, I thought this was over a long time ago. Didn't you two get back together.

CONNIE. For a hot minute and then Lucia decided she would crash my car into Sedutto's ice cream shop on New Dorp Lane.

LUCIA. That's because Connie decided she was gonna sleep with Patti Frizalone after we got back together.

CONNIE. We never said we were exclusive.

LUCIA. You're trash!

*(***MAURIZIO*** *grabs them and pulls them tight.*)*

MAURIZIO. Listen to me ladies, this is not the time or the place, I have enough to worry about with the brothers.

CONNIE. Oh my God is the brother here?

LUCIA. You met him, Connie! Peter, remember?

CONNIE. Yes! Oh my God, they look alike even more now!

LUCIA. Not at all.

CONNIE. Identical.

LUCIA. Not even close.

CONNIE. They could be fuckin' twins!

(**ANTHONY** *enters.*)

Anthony! I'm here, baby. Listen to me, if you need anything I'm right here, okay? Don't worry.

ANTHONY. Thank you Connie.

PETER. Thank you for coming, we met years ago, I'm Peter.

CONNIE. I'm so sorry for your loss, Peter. I'm Connie Scuccifuffio. I've heard such…nice things about you.

PETER. I'm sure.

CONNIE. I need a cigarette.

LUCIA. You went back to smokin'?

CONNIE. How you think I lost the weight?

(**CONNIE** *goes to smoke.* **DOMINICK** *re-enters with a fruit basket.*)

DOMINICK. Look, Mrs. Pinnunziato. Someone sent a beautiful fruit basket.

MAURIZIO. I told Sal, Steve or whatever the hell his name is no more fruit baskets.

ONDINE. Does it have the crackers in it with the nice jellies?

TONIANN. Those apples look divine, Angela! How ripe!

MAURIZIO. Lovely! Would you like to go make a pie with the rest of them downstairs?

ANGELA. Who is it from, Toniann?

TONIANN. Let me look.

(**TONIANN** *goes to open the card…*)

MAURIZIO. I don't care if it's from the Queen of England! It's tacky and hideous and will not sit in this room on my watch.

(**MAURIZIO** *takes it and storms off with it.*)

ANGELA. Oh my God! The Limos.

ANTHONY & PETER. I took care of it!

ANTHONY. Who did you call?

PETER. Sonny Scungili on Amboy Road. Who did you call?

ANTHONY. Anthony Cavallo from Tidy Auto. Sonny Scungili's limo's are so old they still have cigarette stains in them from the seventies.

PETER. Anthony Cavallo's limos are for weddings! Did you get the one with the hot tub?

ANTHONY. No, I got the ones with the dark lights so I don't have to see you and your boyfriend's ugly face any more than I do right now!

ANGELA. Stop it! That's it! I warned you once and I'm not going to say it again!

TONIANN. What the hell is the matter with you two?

MAURIZIO. What the hell happened?

TONIANN. Come on, let's hash it out right now.

ANTHONY. This is not the time or the place.

TONIANN. So we're just gonna make it the elephant in the room for the next three days.

MAURIZIO. Not on my watch!

TONIANN. Everything can be fixed boys. Your Uncle Paulie dumped me on New Year's Eve at 11:59 pm at the Royal Jelly in Atlantic City, for a transvestite! And I forgave him, right Angela?

ANTHONY. There are people here who have come to pay their respects to my father. We are not the only ones who lost someone and unlike my brother who is too selfish to think of anyone else but himself I need to be there for the people that loved my father and who have taken the time to come here.

MARIA. No one is here yet Anthony.

PETER. He doesn't want to talk about it and neither do I.

ANGELA. I demand you boys fix this now!

(*An* **ASIAN WOMAN** *enters.* **MAURIZIO** *leads her to the kneeler.*)

ANTHONY. Mom, calm down. Stop making a scene. Look who is here.

ONDINE. Oh my God, she looks devastated.

ANTHONY. She is.

ANGELA. Who the hell is that?

ANTHONY. She was a good friend of Daddy's.

PETER. I never saw her before in my life.

ANTHONY. That's because you were only around Daddy when you needed something! I knew all his friends. Now if you will excuse me, someone needs to show some respect in this family.

(*The* **ASIAN WOMAN** *is at the kneeler and demonstrates no emotion whatsoever. She sits there still.*)

ANTHONY. I know how hard this is for you. I want you to know how happy my father would be to know that you came today.

EVA. What his name?

(**ANTHONY** *tries not to embarass himself and gets close to her, almost like a whisper.*)

ANTHONY. Joseph.

EVA. Joseph who?

ANTHONY. Pinnunziato.

EVA. Oh! NO! Kung Pao chicken extra spicy. Awww.

ANTHONY. Who are you?

EVA. Eva Fong Onshui from Crown Palace.

ANTHONY. Why are you here?

EVA. Lady call me, Ondine, she say come here now very important, everyone needs me. So maybe you want me to take your order?

(**ANTHONY** *covers and now speaks up for everyone else's benefit.*)

ANTHONY. Yes, Eva. There are things in life we can't explain, and this is just one of those things. I know you and Daddy were very close and I know he would be so happy if he knew you came here to pay your respects.

EVA. Huh?

ANTHONY. Thank you so much for coming! Maurizio, will you please help Eva out, she's a little overwhelmed.

MAURIZIO. Of course! I speak fourteen languages and Mandarin is one of them.

EVA. Zhèxiē rén shì fēngle! *(These people are crazy!)*

MAURIZIO. I know.

(MAURIZIO escorts her out. Everyone looks to ANTHONY, baffled.)

ANTHONY. She'll never get over this.

(RABBI HOWIE HOROWITZ enters.)

ONDINE. Oh look it's Rabbi Howie Horowitz, he performed the Finkelstein boy's bar mitzvah, he was flawless.

TONIANN. Who, the Finkelstein boy or the Rabbi?

ANGELA. What difference does it make? What's he doing here?

(MAURIZIO enters back in and ANGELA pulls him aside.)

ANGELA. Maurizio, can I speak to you. I'm guessing you forgot but we are Catholic and we must have Father…

MAURIZIO. I remember oh too well Mommy, Father Rosalia must perform the service and have no fear, I have already contacted him and he will be available and at the church on Wednesday.

ANGELA. Okay, thank you. So, who is that?

MAURIZIO. That is what the Jewish people call a Rabbi.

ANGELA. We don't know any Rabbis! What's he doing here?

MAURIZIO. Allow me to facilitate this. Please go back and sit and mourn. Try and look more sad and less concerned.

(MAURIZIO goes over to the Rabbi who is now with MARIA.)

MARIA. Maurizio, this is Rabbi Howie Horowitz.

MAURIZIO. A pleasure to meet you, Sir Rabbi. May I ask what brings you here?

HOWIE. Maria?

MARIA. I guess now is a good time. Mom, before everyone gets here I wanted to take a minute to tell you something that I should of told you sooner.

(**MARIA** *pulls her Mother aside and whispers…*)

I'm pregnant.

ANGELA. You're what?

MARIA. *(whispers again)* I'm pregnant.

ANGELA. I can't hear you Maria, please would you just say it already.

MAURIZIO. She's knocked up, Mommy!

MARIA. Mom! I'm pregnant and Howie is the father.

(**ANGELA** *hyperventilates.* **TONIANN** *and* **ONDINE** *fan her.*)

ANGELA. I'm coming in Joe!

MAURIZIO. Someone call 911!

TONIANN. She's fine. Just get me some water please.

ONDINE. This poor woman! I don't know how much more stress she can take.

TONIANN. Where is Angie Cuco now when I need her!

MARIA. Mom! I can't believe you are acting like this!? Can't you be happy for me?

TONIANN. Sweetie, I think your Mom is just a little overwhelmed. This may not have been the best time for that announcement.

ANTHONY. Ya think?

PETER. Oh I know, Anthony, your timing is always perfect!

HOWIE. I really didn't want to cause any extra stress on the family at such a hard time, I should go.

MARIA. Absolutely not! Mom, you have to listen to me. I wanted to tell you when I found out but I didn't want to stress out you and Daddy when he was sick.

ANGELA. So you wait till he's dead! Now I get to deal with this all by myself.

MARIA. You're kidding me! You have two gay sons and you accept them. One even got married and you threw the whole wedding!

TONIANN. You did always say, Angela, you wanted a Grandchild. Now you will have one! A child of God no less!

ONDINE. I heard Billy Crystal is Jewish!

ANGELA. Maria! I wish you would have prepared me for this!

PETER. Mom, just calm down.

ANGELA. I'm not calm. I just lost my husband, I have two gay sons who hate each other and now my daughter is pregnant by a Rabbi. Can this day get any worse!?

*(**EVA** comes storming into the room. She screams hysterically in Chinese.)*

EVA. Youren toule wǒ de ju! Youren toule wǒ de ju! *(Someone stole my car! Someone stole my car!)*

MAURIZIO. Okay, it's one of two things! Either her car has been towed and she thinks it was stolen, or her water broke! I'm going with the first one.

ONDINE. Oh my God, see Angela, you jinxed it, it can get worse.

ANGELA. I don't even know this woman!

LUCIA. I got it. Eva right? I'll get her to a phone.

MAURIZIO. What? You don't even speak Mandarin!?

LUCIA. How do you know?

*(**MAURIZIO** and **LUCIA** take her outside.)*

ANGELA. Maria, I love you, but this is just not the time to discuss this.

HOWIE. She's right Maria, let me go so you can spend some time with your family.

MARIA. But I need you here for support.

ONDINE. Don't worry my love, I am here and I'm not going anywhere.

TONIANN. We are all here, Maria.

HOWIE. I'll come back.

(*HOWIE exits.*)

MARIA. I can't believe you did that!

ANGELA. We will discuss this later. I need to sit down.

TONIANN. Let's go easy on your Mother, okay?

(*MAURIZIO enters.*)

MAURIZIO. Miss Eva has called someone and they are coming to pick her up. I calmed her down and she is outside getting some air.

ONDINE. Oh that poor woman.

ANGELA. Oh fuck her!

TONIANN. Angela!

DOMINICK. I don't think it's the right time for me to be here, Peter.

PETER. When will it be?

DOMINICK. Look what your family is going through?

PETER. I need you with me in case it gets ugly.

MAURIZIO. I am so appalled! The owner of the funeral home just told me that there is a full bar available for the family downstairs. Do the Italian people serve liquor in the Funeral Home?

ANTHONY. I've never heard of such a thing!

MARIA. Mom, I can not believe you made my Howie leave!

ANGELA. Maria, you're pregnant by a Rabbi! You're Catholic and he's going to want you to convert!

MARIA. I already did!

MAURIZIO. Perhaps a nice merlot.

ANGELA. You have got to be kidding me!

TONIANN. Just think of the good stuff, Angela. Now we get to celebrate double the holidays...Christmas AND Cha-noo-ka!

ANGELA. It's Hanukah!

ONDINE. I love Jewish deli.

TONIANN. The one on Father Capodanno has a reuben that will make your head spin it's so good!

ANGELA. Why did everyone wait for Joseph to drop dead and leave me with everything? Did I deserve this?

ONDINE. He's here with us in spirit, Angela.

TONIANN. Oh please, he's at the racetrack in spirit. Sorry.

MARIA. Daddy knew. I told him before he passed away. We went to see him the day he died and he gave us his blessing.

ANGELA. He was on morphine!

TONIANN. Calm down, Angela!

PETER. If Daddy were here he would have supported this. He supported all of us.

ANTHONY. Oh I don't know about this, Peter.

PETER. Oh Anthony, stop!!! The only one in this family who holds grudges is you. The rest of us take what curve balls God throws at us and we deal with it. Life is too short to not be happy.

ANTHONY. There are plenty of people who stabbed Daddy in the back and he never spoke to them again.

ANGELA. Not family Anthony!

ANTHONY. Oh really! When was the last time he spoke to Uncle Vinny? Last time I saw him I was five! I don't see him here do you?

ANGELA. So learn from his mistakes! Is that how you want to live your life? Should we all spend our days walking around with an ax to grind?

PETER. Anthony is the only one who still has an ax to grind over something that happened years ago!

ANGELA. This is not the time nor the place for this conversation.

LUCIA. Anthony seriously. You need to drop this for your father's sake.

MARIA. Listen to her, Anthony.

TONIANN. It was a long time ago honey, people make mistakes.

ONDINE. What happened, Anthony? Let's talk about it.

ANGELA. With all due respect Ondine, can you mind your own business?

ANTHONY. No Ondine, you have a right to know what happened.

PETER. Oh please Ondine, there are two sides to this story.

ANTHONY. His and the truth!

MAURIZIO. Shots anyone?

ANTHONY. Let's call it what it is Peter, the only reason you're with Dominick Vitale still is to hurt me!

MAURIZIO. Let's just move the bar up here.

DOMINICK. Can we not go there, seriously Anthony, not now.

(MAURIZIO gives ANTHONY a shot and he downs it.)

ANTHONY. Picture it, Bay Ridge, 1998, Spectrum!

PETER. Oh please Sophia! I can't believe you still remember this?

ANTHONY. Every single detail.

(Transition music begins to play as the funeral home quickly transforms to a bar. Chairs can move away and lighting can help create the illusion of a dance floor. Main characters move out and drag queen #1 (VIDAL) quickly enters stage center lip syncing a producer's choice song.* As he begins her drag number all main characters make quick costume changes into something more timely and youthful.)

---

* Please see Music Use Note on page 3.

SCENE II – SPECTRUM NIGHT CLUB

(As selected song [producer's choice]* creates the transition from funeral home to nightclub. There are three time transitions here that are all in the same night. In the first part of the flashback we see **CONNIE** *and* **LUCIA** *enter first as quite the happy couple. We establish* **EZIO** *[from offstage] as the bartender.)*

CONNIE. Come on, babe! Let's do Jell-o shots!

LUCIA. You are out of your mind with these Jell-O Shots! Laurie Cipullo is a bad influence.

CONNIE. Babe! I just had a week from hell I need to loosen up tonight.

LUCIA. You drove tonight!

CONNIE. We can sober up at the Americana Diner across the street later! What the hell with this beeper it keeps going off. *(She looks.)* Friggin' Patti Testaverde everything is 911 911.

LUCIA. Oh my God, you better call her!

CONNIE. There is a line for the pay phone a mile long!

LUCIA. What do you think she wants?

CONNIE. She probably wants to know what time France Joli is singing. You know Patti, she always has to be on a fuckin' schedule!

LUCIA. Those beepers are so annoying. Seriously, we managed just fine without them.

CONNIE. Oh wait babe! Look Dimondelle Dupree is coming on!

*(Diamondelle, our resident drag queen, [***VIDAL***] comes out in full drag regalia and performs a drag number [producer's choice]*. When complete the girls and* **EZIO** *applaud and* **ANTHONY** *enters. Diamondelle thanks the girls, greets* **ANTHONY** *and exits.)*

ANTHONY. What's up, my favorite girls on the planet! Wow, it's packed tonight!

---

*Please see Music Use Note on page 3.

LUCIA. That's cause France Joli is singing tonight.

ANTHONY. Oh I love her!

CONNIE. How is my baby doin'!?

LUCIA. How did it go? I want full details.

CONNIE. Oh my God the one year anniversary dinner was tonight?

ANTHONY. No words!

LUCIA. Where did you go?

ANTHONY. He took me to "One If By Land…"

ANTHONY/LUCIA. "TWO IF BY SEA!"

CONNIE. I love that place!

LUCIA. When were you there?

CONNIE. Back in the day babe, back in the day.

ANTHONY. Well I highly recommend. It was so romantic and the ambience in the village was just incredible. You girls should go there for your one year anniversary.

CONNIE. I'll take you, honey.

LUCIA. Awww, where is he?

ANTHONY. He just stopped to say hello to John and Jay, oh here he is!

(**DOMINICK** *enters*)

DOMINICK. Miss me?

(**ANTHONY** *and* **DOMINICK** *kiss passionately.*)

ANTHONY. Are you sure we can chase a Jell-o shot after two lemon drop shots?

CONNIE. Vodka base babe! You're good.

LUCIA. What about the Jolly Rancher shots?

CONNIE. That's vodka base!

LUCIA. Are you boys gonna do a little hustle.

CONNIE. Oh my God it's the cutest thing! Wait for Donna Bianco to get here.

LUCIA. Where is she?

CONNIE. Please, she's been on her way for an hour, that bitch is always late.

(**PETER** *enters discreetly upstage and has his back turned so his face is not visible.*)

LUCIA. Oh my God Anthony, that guy looks so familiar! Isn't that your roommate from Fire Island?

ANTHONY. No, it's…it's my brother.

CONNIE. Shut the fuck up!

LUCIA. What's he doing here?

CONNIE. I knew he had a gay vibe!

ANTHONY. He swears he's not!

LUCIA. Then why is he here…by himself!

DOMINICK. Are you okay? Should we leave?

ANTHONY. I'm certainly not gonna leave, but if he sees me he might.

LUCIA. Are you shocked?

ANTHONY. Not at all!

DOMINICK. You always said you thought it was possible.

ANTHONY. My parents are very funny with the whole gay thing still, but I mean I kind of broke the ice.

DOMINICK. I thought your Mom said he had girlfriends?

ANTHONY. Yeah, I have girlfriends too, Connie and Lucia! Doesn't mean I'm sleeping with them.

(**PETER** *turns and sees* **ANTHONY** *and starts to make a bee-line out.* **ANTHONY** *immediately goes after and pulls him by his jacket.*)

ANTHONY. Not so fast!

PETER. It's not what you think.

ANTHONY. And what do I think!?

PETER. I'm not like you. I just came here to meet someone.

ANTHONY. Oh really, you drove over the bridge to the only gay bar in the area to meet….Who?

PETER. My friend.

ANTHONY. Your friend who?

PETER. Joe.

ANTHONY. Joe?

PETER. Joe…leen. Joleen. It's a blind date.

ANTHONY. You have a blind date with a girl named Joleen in a gay bar in Brooklyn?

PETER. I didn't know it was a gay bar.

ANTHONY. Peter…stop. Why would you think you can't talk to me? If anyone is not gonna judge you, it's me.

PETER. You have no idea what I'm going through, Anthony!

ANTHONY. Yes I do know! I went through the same thing.

PETER. This could ruin my whole career!

ANTHONY. You're a hairdresser.

PETER. Exactly! What will people think!?

ANTHONY. That it's about time.

PETER. Anthony, I'm serious! What are my clients gonna do when they find out their hairdresser is gay!

ANTHONY. Pay double. Peter, seriously…there is a whole world outside of Staten Island. Mommy and Daddy will understand, they may need some time but they will.

PETER. This is gonna kill Mommy.

ANTHONY. Mommy is not gonna be too shocked. Trust me!

PETER. You think she knows?

ANTHONY. Considering you had the New Kids On The Block taped all over your wall as a kid, you were the lead singer in the chorus in high school and you dropped out of college to go to hair school. I would say it might have passed her mind once! Who did you come here with?

PETER. I came alone.

ANTHONY. Oh my God. Come meet my friends.

(ANTHONY *brings* PETER *over to* DOMINICK, CONNIE *and* LUCIA.)

ANTHONY. Guys, this is my brother. Peter.

LUCIA. We met at the Christmas party at the bowling alley!

CONNIE. So is this your coming out party tonight?

LUCIA. Connie!

CONNIE. What?

ANTHONY. Dominick, you've met Peter.

DOMINICK. Nice to see you here finally!

PETER. Finally?

DOMINICK. Anthony always said you were in the closet.

ANTHONY. *(coughs)* Wait till you hear France Joli sing tonight! She's unbelievable.

PETER. I'm sorry I always act so weird around you. It's just this whole gay thing...I guess I was just scared... confused...

ANTHONY. Peter look, you already have a support group!

PETER. This is so weird, I feel like I'm gonna throw up. I'm so nervous being in a gay bar.

CONNIE. You need a shot!

LUCIA. Everything is a shot.

ANTHONY. I think Connie is right, we can all use a shot right now.

CONNIE. *(calls off)* Ezio babe, tequila shots all around!

LUCIA. Tequila now!???

CONNIE. It's vodka based!

LUCIA. This is gonna be some night!

(The music transitions to a line dance song and the drag queen returns and leads the line. As the drag queen is doing her thing...LUCIA, CONNIE, ANTHONY, PETER and DOMINICK are doing shots in the background at Ezio's bar, laughing and having a great time trying to follow along.)

DOMINICK. I'm feeling this tonight! Peter, you know how to do it?

PETER. Oh I can't dance.

ANTHONY. Show him Dominick!

DOMINICK. Yes you can! Come on I'll teach you.

(LUCIA, CONNIE and ANTHONY cheer as DOMINICK and PETER make their way to the downstage center area where DOMINICK leads PETER in what starts as

innocent dancing but their attraction is palpable. As the dancing continues it turns more and more intense. **ANTHONY** *is getting lit in the background and is oblivious to what is happening. The boys continue to dance while the drag queen drifts off, as do* **PETER** *and* **DOMINICK**.)

CONNIE. Anthony! I think Ezio the mint-looking bartender is digging you!

LUCIA. Troublemaker, why you got to point it out?

CONNIE. Babe! I'm just saying we haven't paid for one drink!

LUCIA. Connie stop, you'll get Ezio in trouble!

CONNIE. Chill out, babe! I'm just pointing out the obvi!

ANTHONY. Well it doesn't matter cause Dominick is my soulmate!

LUCIA. Awwwww! He calls Anthony his little nutella muffin.

ANTHONY. I die.

LUCIA. I die.

ANTHONY/LUCIA. I die!

CONNIE. Why am I the only one not wasted?!

ANTHONY. I'm still dying that Jay had Tony Leone thrown out of the club!

LUCIA. Now, he was wasted!

CONNIE. Jay looked pissed!

ANTHONY. Crazy shit happens when people get drunk. Then tomorrow everyone gets over it.

CONNIE. True that!

LUCIA. Where is your brother?

ANTHONY. Dominick took him to the bar to use the pay phone. My mother was beeping him.

LUCIA. Oh My God, that is not gonna be pretty.

ANTHONY. She'll be fine. When she wakes up tomorrow I'll give her a few xanax and she'll get over it.

LUCIA. So how are you doing really?

ANTHONY. Honestly, I'm still just taking it all in. It's one thing when, you know, it's another thing to have it in front of you and figure out how to deal with it the right way.

LUCIA. I get it.

ANTHONY. I just don't want him to fall in with the wrong crowd. He's my little brother, I love him.

LUCIA. Please! I know what you mean, but we will be here, we will take him out with us. And hopefully after he figures it all out, he will meet a nice guy and fall in love like we all did.

CONNIE. Let's do a shot!

LUCIA. Seriously Connie, how are you still able to walk?

CONNIE. Babe! It's a big night, lots to celebrate! Anthony come on…

ANTHONY. No more shots! Just get me a Long Island Iced Tea.

CONNIE/LUCIA/ANTHONY. Vodka base!

(Final music transition. Drag Queen #1 comes out and lip syncs a current 1998 song.* This should now be around 2 am where clearly everyone is intoxicated. After the drag queen performs, lights up on **PETER** *and* **DOMINICK** *making out on the opposite side of the stage.* **ANTHONY, CONNIE** *and* **LUCIA** *slowly notice.* **ANTHONY** *drops his drink, conflicted, he stands there in shock.* **LUCIA** *grabs his arms not sure what to do or what to say.)*

LUCIA. Anthony, they're both drunk.

(ANTHONY *walks towards both of them. He shoots a look of disappointment to* **DOMINICK** *and then a very powerful look to* **PETER**.*)*

ANTHONY. You're dead to me.

(blackout)

---

*Please see Music Use Note on page 3.

ACT TWO

FUNERAL HOME

(Day two of the wake. Funeral home is set as it was. **LUCIA** *is with* **ANTHONY** *on one side of the stage helping with the flowers and* **PETER** *is with* **DOMINICK** *on the other doing busywork as well. There is still tension in the room.* **MARIA** *and* **ANGELA** *are at the kneeler.* **ONDINE** *enters and barrels her way right in the middle putting her arms around both of them.* **MAURIZIO** *enters.)*

MAURIZIO. Hello Everyone! I see we all made it back for day two. Ondine you are early…again.

ONDINE. Oh Maurizio, with all that traffic on Hylan Boulevard, I knew I had to leave extra early so I could be here for the family.

ANGELA. Thank you!

MAURIZIO. Lucia, I am hoping you and Connie will be on good behavior today.

LUCIA. She actually has to work today, but she will be here for the funeral tomorrow. We had a long conversation last night and realized we had to put our differences aside for Anthony.

PETER. Of course! Anthony is the only one who needs support.

ANTHONY. Oh I'm sorry Peter, stealing my boyfriend wasn't enough you want my friends too?

ANGELA. What did I say to you two last night?! You promised you were going to both be on your best behavior. Now cut it, I mean it. Maurizio, the boys are also going to be putting their differences aside because they know that is what their father would want.

MAURIZIO. Fabulous! I will have Sal put the bar away today since now I know there will be no drama in this room.

(**TONIANN** *enters with her Starbucks in hand.*)

TONIANN. I wouldn't go that far Maurizio.

(**ONDINE** *rushes over to her.*)

ONDINE. Toniann, how are you holding up?

TONIANN. Barely, Ondine. You will never guess who called me last night.

ONDINE. Who?

TONIANN. Angela's sister-in-law, Donna

ANGELA. Donna!!

ONDINE. Oh my God I didn't even think of her! Oh Toniann, she must be devastated.

TONIANN. Devastated isn't even the word, she had me on the phone all morning.

ONDINE. Did you give her the arrangements?

TONIANN. Yes, she will be here today.

ANGELA. Toniann, I purposely waited to tell her hoping she wouldn't come! She's always too cheap to fly in from Tampa but now give her a chance to play the martyr and she's on the next flight!

TONIANN. Oh Angela, please! Donna was Joe's sister!

MARIA. I love Aunt Donna!

ANGELA. She's a pain in the ass!

TONIANN. Oh God Angela, she's hasn't lived here in twenty years, how much drama could she cause?

ANGELA. Just wait!

TONIANN. Well Donna is taking it very bad.

ONDINE. That poor woman!

TONIANN. I don't even know if I can be in the room when she gets here. It's too much.

(**PETER** *crosses over.*)

PETER. Well I have some good news since I know we all can use some.

ANTHONY. Of course it's gotta be all about him.

LUCIA. Calm down.

PETER. Dominick and I are getting married.

(Everyone is speechless.)

MAURIZIO. So much for closing the bar today!

ANGELA. Peter, even I have to say this is not the time for this.

ANTHONY. Ya think?

LUCIA. You want to go outside and get some air?

ANTHONY. Oh no, this I have to hear.

PETER. I'm sorry, I told Daddy before he passed away and he left me money for the wedding. He felt since Anthony had a big wedding he thought it was only fair…

ANTHONY. You have got to be kidding me.

MARIA. What about my wedding? Daddy said he was going to leave me money to get married too! My wedding has to come first Peter I mean I'm pregnant, let's be fair.

ONDINE. You could do a double wedding! Oh how glorious that would be!

TONIANN. A gay wedding and a Jewish wedding? Oh my God I really wouldn't know what to wear.

ANGELA. Maria, this is not about you right now, it's about Peter. This is very happy news, Peter, and I know your father just wanted you to be happy.

DOMINICK. I love him Angela.

ANGELA. I know you do, Dominick. *(to **ANTHONY**)* Everyone deserves happiness.

PETER. Thanks Mom! And Mom, will you give me away?

*(**MAURIZIO** places his hand on **ANTHONY**'s mouth again.)*

ANGELA. Of course I will Peter! I did it for Anthony and I will do it for you. Where will you having the wedding?

PETER. Aruba. I want to do a destination wedding with just fifty people.

ANGELA. I think that's perfect!

ANTHONY. *(to* **LUCIA***)* Leave it him to have everyone flying all over hell and back to watch him get married.

DOMINICK. We are going to have just our closest friends.

ANTHONY. *(to* **LUCIA***)* They don't have any.

DOMINICK. And of course our family. My mother will be giving me away as well.

ANTHONY. *(to* **LUCIA***)* And then everyone's got to pay for hotel and airfare and an envelope.

MAURIZIO. If you need a wedding coordinator...

(**ANTHONY** *yanks his arm.*)

my rates are double what they were ten years ago.

ANTHONY. *(to* **LUCIA***)* I bet Father Rosalia doesn't need to perform this service!

ANGELA. Since it's in Aruba who are you going to have perform the wedding?

PETER. Just a regular minister.

ANGELA. Oh how perfect!

(**MAURIZIO** *and* **LUCIA** *both cover* **ANTHONY***'s mouth.* **PETER** *crosses over to* **ANTHONY***.)*

PETER. And Anthony, it would mean so much to me if you would put our differences aside and you and Andrew attended.

ANTHONY. Don't even waste an invitation.

PETER. See Mom, I tried.

ANGELA. Oh Anthony, let it go!

ANTHONY. And I'm the bad guy, again!

DOMINICK. Anthony, it would mean so much to Peter and that's what your father would want!

ANTHONY. Don't you dare stand there and tell me what my father would have wanted!

PETER. Don't even bother Dominick, it's pointless.

ANTHONY. The only reason you're doing this is to be a spiteful little bitch because Daddy threw me a wedding first!

(PETER steps to ANTHONY.)

PETER. Oh and where is Andrew? What kind of "husband" doesn't show up when his father-in-law drops dead!

(ANTHONY is visibly pissed and lunges for his throat, as LUCIA and MAURIZIO hold him back…in walks DONNA DICECCO who screams from the door.)

DONNA. Joey!!! Joey!!! Oh God how could you do this to me! Joey!

ONDINE. Oh my God it's the sister!

MAURIZIO. Perfect time for Aunt Donna!

ANGELA. Here she goes!

TONIANN. Donna sit down!

ONDINE. Do you need water?

DONNA. I want to see him. *(She makes her way to the coffin.)* The flight was horrible! Turbulence! I screamed and screamed but no one even cared.

ANGELA. I'm surprised they didn't land the plane just for you.

DONNA. I know! I couldn't believe it either!

ONDINE. Are you sure you can handle this, Donna?

DONNA. No! I am not sure I can handle this…person! But I'm gonna try! For my brother.

(TONIANN and ONDINE walk her over to the coffin. She is visibly shaken and hysterical. She is completely over the top and very dramatic as she slowly but finally gets to the coffin.)

DONNA. Oh Joey! Oh Joey!

TONIANN. Angela. get her water.

ANGELA. Get HER water?

MARIA. I'll get it.

ANTHONY. I got it.

PETER. Aunt Donna's my Godmother, I will get it!

TONIANN. You're so good Peter. Thank you!

ONDINE. Donna I would have called you if I had your number. Angie Cuco told me yesterday morning when I was having my coffee and I was shocked.

DONNA. Was he sick?

ANGELA. For four years!

DONNA. And how come no one called me!?

ANTHONY. Aunt Donna I left a ton of messages on your cell phone.

DONNA. Oh Anthony baby I had to shut the cell phone, AT&T raised the rates through the roof!

ANGELA. But she could afford to go to Vegas twice a year.

(**DONNA** *goes to* **ANGELA**.)

DONNA. No one should have to go through this Angela. I don't know how you will ever move on.

ANGELA. Thank you.

MAURIZIO. Please miss can you sit down, the family has a lot going on right now.

ANGELA. I'm done! I'm done talking about my kids weddings and why they don't speak. Let's remember your father right now. *Capisce!?*

DONNA. Oh I have something for you Angela, I left it in the car. Excuse me.

(*She starts to exit and walks perfectly without the cane till she catches herself.*)

DONNA. Owwww!!! My cane! My cane!

(*They hand her the cane and she walks out limping again.*)

MAURIZIO. So not to bring up another hot topic but we simply must address the eulogy. Has there been any discussion as to who is going to do it?

ANGELA. An excellent question, Maurizio!

MAURIZIO. Volunteers?

(PETER and ANTHONY exchange looks, ANGELA looks to both of them. ONDINE gets up.)

ONDINE. Angela, if you want me to give the eulogy I will.

ANGELA. Thank you Ondine, but I would like it to be one or all of his children.

MARIA. Well I'm already singing at the funeral.

MAURIZIO. Again! What??!! How did this happen?

ANGELA. You're singing at the funeral?

MARIA. Daddy loved the way I sang and THAT will be my eulogy.

TONIANN. I think that's beautiful Maria. What are you going to sing?

MARIA. "Papa can you hear me? Papa can you see me?"

MAURIZIO. *Yentl?*

TONIANN. Wow this Jewish thing is really going right to her head.

PETER. Anthony can give the eulogy.

ANTHONY. Oh how convenient! I absolutely will not.

PETER. Oh My God I can't win with you!

(DONNA comes in with a tray of eggplant.)

DONNA. Angela, I brought you a peace offering.

ANGELA. What the hell is it?

DONNA. My famous eggplant that you love. But I want my tin back.

ONDINE. Oh my God I'm gonna cry!

ANGELA. That wasn't necessary Donna.

DONNA. Look! I know we haven't always been on the best of terms. But you have raised beautiful children even though I may not have always agreed with some of your parenting decisions. Lucky for you you had Joseph and they all turned out lovely. I think my brother would be very proud.

(**HOWIE** *enters.*)

HOWIE. Good afternoon.

DONNA. Oh I'm sorry Rabbi, you must be in the wrong room.

MARIA. No Aunt Donna, this is my fiancee Rabbi Howie Horowitz.

DONNA. WHAT!???

MARIA. He's a wonderful man Aunt Donna and we're having a baby.

DONNA. You're pregnant with his baby? You're not even married!

HOWIE. We are getting married right away. Maria has already converted to Judiasm and you have my word that your niece and our baby will be well taken care of.

DONNA. What! Is everyone trying to kill me!? Angela, tell me you won't allow this!

ANGELA. Do I have a choice?!

DONNA. My brother would never allow this!

MARIA. I told him Aunt Donna, before he died.

HOWIE. He gave us his blessing.

DONNA. I don't believe that for one second! Angela this is all your fault! *Sei una disgraziata!*

(**DONNA** *takes back the eggplant.*)

ANGELA. *Statazit* you pain in the ass!

TONIANN. Ladies! Ladies please! There is no need to let a good eggplant go to waste.

(**TONIANN** *takes the eggplant and puts it away.* **DONNA** *goes and sits away from* **ANGELA.** **ONDINE** *and* **TONIANN** *sit in the middle so they are divided.* **LUCIA** *goes over to* **DOMINICK** *while* **ANTHONY** *is with* **MAURIZIO** *and* **PETER** *is with* **HOWIE** *and* **MARIA.**)

LUCIA. Dominick, do you have a second?

DOMINICK. Hey, Lucia.

LUCIA. Look, I know how awkward this is for you.

DOMINICK. This is like the most awkward place I've ever been.

LUCIA. I know. Look, I want this to go away for Anthony as much as you want it to go away for Peter.

DOMINICK. I want it to get better for both of them.

LUCIA. I think they are both taking this very bad. But it's times like this everyone just has to bury the hatchet and learn to forgive and move on.

DOMINICK. I don't know what more I can do on my end but I'm open to anything.

(*LUCIA calls over to* **MAURIZIO**.)

LUCIA. Maurizio, is there anything we can do to help this situation. We feel terrible.

MAURIZIO. Relax, my lipstick lesbian. I have already been in contact with someone who can help us.

DOMINICK. Who?

MAURIZIO. As you know I am very well connected in the global network of last-minute solutions. I placed a phone call last night.

LUCIA. To who?

MAURIZIO. He should be here any second.

(*enter* **VIDAL**)

VIDAL. Maurizio!

MAURIZIO. There he is! Vidal!

(*They air kiss.*)

LUCIA/DOMINICK. Vidal?

MAURIZIO. Je vous remercie beaucoup d'etre venu Vidal! Ces personnes ont besoin de votre aide! (*Thank you so much for coming Vidal, these people need your help!*)

VIDAL. J'ai annule tous mes rendez-vous juste pour vous! (*I canceled all my appointments just for you.*)

MAURIZIO. Oh *Merci, Merci!*

ANGELA. What, are we in the United Nations? Who the hell is this now?

MAURIZIO. Allow me to introduce you all, I have invited someone in to make a very special call today. I am sure many of you know the very famous Vidal!

ANGELA. Sassoon?

MAURIZIO. No, but I know him too. This is Vidal Dubois.

TONIANN. Oh my God the psychic!

VIDAL. I am not a psychic! I am a medium.

LUCIA. I heard of you! You're in the west village!

TONIANN. Oh my God I have been trying get an appointment with you for years.

MAURIZIO. Yes, and as you can tell Vidal's time is very valuable. So we must begin right away.

ANTHONY. Maurizio, I am confused why he's here...

MAURIZIO. Well, of course, to speak to your father. I wanted to see if any of you had any questions for the deceased and Vidal can channel.

ANGELA. Oh, I don't know where to start!

MARIA. I have so many questions!

ONDINE. Me too!

VIDAL. Silence!

(VIDAL approaches the casket.)

VIDAL. Before I begin, I must first connect with the spirit and make sure he is present and wants to come through the portal.

(VIDAL does some over-the-top ritual to summon the spirit.)

VIDAL. The spirit is with us.

ONDINE. Oh Thank Jesus!

DONNA. Joe!

ANGELA. Oh my God!

ANTHONY. *(skeptic)* Really?

LUCIA. Let him do this Anthony.

VIDAL. What are your questions for Joseph?

TONIANN. Holy Shit! He knew his name.

ANTHONY. It's in the casket!

ANGELA. I want to know who and what he wants for a eulogy. We never discussed that.

ONDINE. Ask him if he thinks we should order more donuts on Tuesday Mornings for the ladies league. Liz Dehart says we always run out!

MARIA. Ask him if he is okay with me naming the baby Jonah if it's a boy.

DONNA. Ask him if he's okay that his daughter is now Jewish and his wife continues to disgrace this family!!

TONIANN. Tell him if Gary Gavone still owes him money I will take care of it. Can I keep some of it? I'm broke!

(They look to **ANTHONY**, *who is not buying any of this.)*

ANTHONY. Ask him who is taking over for Barbara Walters on *The View* when she retires. I'm worried.

VIDAL. Too many voices! Too many voices!

MAURIZIO. Everyone shut up, Vidal can not work like this. Vidal, please.

VIDAL. The spirit is calling out for someone.

ANGELA. Who is he calling for?

MAURIZIO. Shhhhhhh!!!

VIDAL. He's calling for someone with an A.

ONDINE. Oh my God he's looking for Angie Cuco!

ANGELA. He's looking for me, you ass! I'm Angela! I'm right here Joe!

VIDAL. It's not a woman he's calling for.

(They look around and realize it's **ANTHONY**.)

ANTHONY. Yup! My name starts with an A!

TONIANN. Your father is trying to talk to you, Anthony.

ANGELA. What's he saying Vidal?

TONIANN. Is it Anthony he wants?

VIDAL. Yes!

DONNA. Oh my God!

ANTHONY. Oh Please! You're telling me he's here and he's yelling the letter A! What's he doing? Watching the *Wheel of Fortune?* I don't believe in this stuff.

ANGELA. Anthony can you be open minded about something for once?

ANTHONY. Give me a break Ma, if Daddy was really talking to this guy he would have a lot more to say than the letter A.

VIDAL. Your father wants to know why you haven't told anyone that you and Andrew are no longer together.

*(They all look to **ANTHONY**.)*

ANGELA. Is that true Anthony?

PETER. Well I'll be damned.

ANTHONY. How did you know that?

VIDAL. Still not a believer?

ONDINE. The gays are allowed to get divorced?

TONIANN. I always say the first time is just practice!

ANGELA. What about the second and the third, Toniann?

TONIANN. More practice?

ANTHONY. *(to **LUCIA**)* Who did you tell? You're the only one who knew?

LUCIA. I swear I didn't tell a soul.

ANGELA. Why didn't you tell anyone Anthony?

ANTHONY. Well, unlike some people I didn't think it was the appropriate time or the place.

ANGELA. After ten years, Anthony?

TONIANN. What happened, Anthony?

ANTHONY. Andrew left me! For a hairdresser!

*(He shoots **PETER** a dirty look.)*

PETER. I am so sorry, Anthony.

ANTHONY. No you're not and don't act like you are.

VIDAL. Ahhhh…the spirit has more to say.

TONIANN. Oh my God what else??

VIDAL. He senses the conflict of his spawn and demands a truce amongst the children. He is saying his soul will not rest till an alliance amongst the kin is formed.

ANGELA. See what you're doing to him Anthony!

MAURIZIO. Vidal, is there anything else?

VIDAL. Unfortunately, there is too much friction in the air for the spirit to continue. I believe my job is done for now.

(VIDAL gets up and extends his card to ANGELA.)

Again, I am sorry for your loss. We can try again if and when the air has been cleared. Maurizio, I must go! Liza Minnelli is coming in later and I need to prepare. That woman gets more visitors than the Pope. *Au Revoir!*

(MAURIZIO air kisses with VIDAL and MARIA shows him out. DOMINICK pulls MAURIZIO aside.)

DOMINICK. That was good, Maurizio. But how did you know about Anthony and Andrew?

MAURIZIO. I didn't.

(MAURIZIO's phone rings.)

MAURIZIO. Excuse me.

ONDINE. Angela, I'm still in shock over all that. I can't imagine how you must feel?

ANGELA. I feel like I want my husband to be happy wherever he is.

MARIA. Can't we all just get along? Howie can you please help my family?

HOWIE. I don't want to overstep but I do think no matter what your beliefs this should be a lesson to everyone that now is a time for forgiveness.

ANTHONY. Speak for yourself.

TONIANN. Well I don't know what the Jews believe but I can tell you this Howie, I smell the *malocchio!*

DONNA. Ahhhhh Malocchio!

ONDINE. And we can't even wear red 'cause it's a funeral!

ANTHONY. Oh please, you seriously believe in that!

LUCIA. My whole family believes in it and so do I.

ANTHONY. Lucia, there is no such thing as an Italian Curse!

(MAURIZIO hangs up the phone and steps forward.)

MAURIZIO. This Father Rosalia is going to be the vein of my ever-loving European existence! He has kidney stones for real this time and he will not be here to do the final prayer or the funeral!

ANGELA. You see what you did Anthony, you put the hex on him!

ONDINE. Ahhhhhh!!

TONIANN. Malocchio!!

ANGELA. Oh my God, Maurizio, this is awful, who is going to replace him?

DONNA. Call Father Fiorello, Maurizio, tell him I sent you.

ANGELA. He died two months ago Donna!

DONNA. What!??? Another knife to the heart!

TONIANN. I went to the funeral with Donatella and Allesia. It was a total tragedy.

DONNA. How did he die Toniann?

TONIANN. Sudden heart attack, to this day no one knows what caused it.

ANGELA. He was ninety-seven!

TONIANN. Such a sin! He took such good care of himself too.

ONDINE. Oh my God! More tragedy! They say it comes in threes.

TONIANN. Yup, first it was Father Fiorello, then Cousin Sonny and now Joseph.

DONNA. Sonny!!!????

TONIANN. Oh my God! No one called you about Sonny. Were you two close?

DONNA. Very! I need some water. I need air.

ANGELA. When the hell were you close with Sonny? You met him twice!

DONNA. We used to chat on Facebook and play Words with Friends. He beat me every time.

ONDINE. I need to take this poor woman outside for some air.

(**DONNA** *sobs hysterically as* **ONDINE** *takes her out screaming the whole way.*)

DONNA. Sonny!!! Sonny!!!!

HOWIE. Mrs. Pinnunziato it would be my honor to say a few words and a prayer for your husband if you need someone.

MAURIZIO. Oh perfect!

ANGELA. I'm sorry Rabbi, but my husband would not want that.

MARIA. Mom, how could you say that?

TONIANN. I don't think he would care, Angela.

ANGELA. I know what my husband would want and he would want a catholic priest.

TONIANN. He never went to church a day in his life! What difference does it make? A man of God is a man of God, whether he's wearing the collar or the beanie!

MAURIZIO. I don't think we can get anyone else on such late notice.

HOWIE. I don't mean to step on toes Mrs. Pinnunziato. I just wanted to offer my help.

ANGELA. That's very nice of you Rabbi, but I just don't feel comfortable with this.

TONIANN. It will send your sister-in-law through the roof!

ANGELA. You're hired!

TONIANN. Atta girl!

(**LUCIA** *takes* **ANTHONY** *aside.*)

LUCIA. Anthony, you know I'm on your side, but maybe you should let this feud go for the sake of your mother. I don't know how much more she can take.

ANTHONY. I don't know how much more she can take either. I don't know how much more I can take.

LUCIA. I know, but seriously, you have to get through the funeral, it would be so much easier if you just made some sort of peace.

ANTHONY. I think the worst is over and tomorrow this will all be over and I will never have to look at either of them again!

(MAURIZIO comes flying back in.)

MAURIZIO. Ladies and Gentlemen please do not panic, there is a hurricane coming!

TONIANN. Malocchio!!!!

MAURIZIO. They have upped it to a category one so we will have to postpone the Funeral.

ANTHONY. *(looks up)* Oh you're good!

TONIANN. What do you mean postpone?

MAURIZIO. It means we are wrapping up this session very soon. The mayor has declared a state of emergency.

TONIANN. But Naz cancelled the Ladies' Classic League tonight just so everyone could come!

MAURIZIO. They can come to the funeral in a few days when I reschedule it.

TONIANN. What about Angie Cuco? She left AC early just to make the wake!

MAURIZIO. Angie Cuco is making me Coo-Coo! Call them all and tell them they will have to come to the funeral instead!

TONIANN. Oh my God I better call all the girls! Leave it to your husband Angela to screw everybody up. Even when he's dead he's a pain in my ass.

(ONDINE enters in panic.)

ONDINE. Oh my God! A hurricane is coming!

MAURIZIO. Thank you, Miss Ondine, we are well aware.

ONDINE. Sal took Donna outside. She is so upset that she lit a cigarette and she said she hasn't had one in ten years.

ANGELA. Oh she's so full of shit!

TONIANN. Angela, please! It was her brother.

ONDINE. Maurizio, what is going to happen with the services?

MAURIZIO. We are cancelling the evening session and the funeral will be when I can reschedule it.

ONDINE. Oh my God!! Angie Cuco!!!

TONIANN. She's in AC. She won't get back in time.

ONDINE. Oh my God this is horrible.

ANGELA. I'll be honest, no offense to Angie Cuco, but I barely know her and I could care less if she's here.

TONIANN. Angela!

MAURIZIO. I think now would be a good time for some final words, because we need to remember a hurricane is coming and they are going to throw us all out of here.

ONDINE. Oh my God! I'll go get Donna!

(ONDINE exits.)

MAURIZIO. Everyone please be seated. Rabbi, please say something meaningful.

(Everyone sits as HOWIE slowly makes his way to the front of the room.)

HOWIE. Well I would like to begin by saying what an honor it is to speak for the man who helped create the woman who I plan to spend the rest of my life with. Without even knowing him, I know that if he raised such an amazing woman like Maria…he must have been a man worth remembering for eternity. As we say in Hebrew…*yitgaddal veyitqaddash shmeh rabba. Be'alma di vra khir'uteh.*

(DONNA and ONDINE enter on the next.)

Veyamlikh malkhuteh. Veyatzmah purqaneh viqarev qetz meshiheh.

(**DONNA** *screams at the site of this and faints in the back.* **ONDINE** *catches her.*)

ONDINE. I don't how much this poor woman can take.

MAURIZIO. Out of the way…

ONDINE. She fainted!

MAURIZIO. Is she breathing?

ONDINE. Barely!

MAURIZIO. Put her in a chair and let's go! We have no time.

ONDINE. Oh my God Angela, should we call an ambulance?

ANGELA. She's fine! She's a hypochondriac, just like her mother was!

DONNA. Don't you dare speak about my mother!

ANGELA. See, I told you she was fine. Rabbi please continue, in English if it's not too much trouble.

HOWIE. Yes of course, well again having never met Joseph I can only speak of what I know of him from Maria. One of the things I admire most about him was his patience and his love of his family. Most men who are like Joseph and of his generation, are not well educated on the things like sexuality. Joseph understood that both his sons were gay, and regardless he loved them both. It takes a real man to find a way to accept when his children are so different. I think Joseph was a role model for parents all over this country and I can only hope that the fathers of our future, including myself, will learn by his example. All of you were very blessed to have been raised by a man who believed in tolerance, acceptance and most of all forgiveness. All families and all walks of life carry grudges in some form or another. It's natural to hurt, but it hurts too much to hate. God did not want us to hate, he wanted us to love and accept the way Joseph did. I may be a stranger to this family but I would like to take this moment to thank God for the life of Joseph, and I want to thank him for teaching all of his children and those around him how powerful it is to love and to be loved. It's something we all want and we all deserve. Thank You.

(**HOWIE** *sits. Everyone is emotional but* **ONDINE** *and* **DONNA** *are over the top hysterical.*)

ONDINE. I haven't cried that much since Luke and Laura's wedding!

DONNA. That was beautiful, Rabbi. Absolutely beautiful. Thank you!

HOWIE. My pleasure.

(**DONNA** *rises and goes to* **ANGELA.**)

DONNA. I know Joseph would not want us to fight.

ANGELA. No he wouldn't.

DONNA. I'm sorry, Angela. I know how much you loved him.

ANGELA. He was the love of my life.

(**DONNA** *and* **ANGELA** *hug and then take a moment and walk over to the coffin together. They kneel and look over him and say a prayer.* **ANGELA** *finally loses it.* **DONNA** *comforts her and walks her out.*)

MAURIZIO. If you are not immediate family would you quickly say goodbye so they can have some time. Keep in mind a hurricane is coming, Ondine.

(*Simultaneously…* **ONDINE, DOMINICK, LUCIA,** *and* **HOWIE** *all start to make their way out.* **ONDINE** *waves farewell to Joseph while* **LUCIA** *hugs* **ANTHONY,** **DOMINICK** *hugs* **PETER** *and* **HOWIE** *hugs* **MARIA.** *They exit.*)

MAURIZIO. Aunt Toniann, shall we give the children some time alone with their father.

TONIANN. Of course.

(**TONIANN** *approaches the casket.*)

Ya know, I never told you this but I did love you…you rat bastard.

(**MAURIZIO** *and* **TONIANN** *exit.*)

*(**PETER**, **MARIA** and **ANTHONY** are left alone. A very awkward moment in the room.)*

MARIA. I have never been as disappointed in both of you as I am today.

PETER. Why?

MARIA. Daddy loved all of us and gave us everything we could ever want his whole life, and this is how you repay him?

ANTHONY. Maria…

MARIA. Don't! I'm carrying your future niece or nephew. If you don't fix this, I prmoise you you will never see me or this baby. I want my child to learn how to love and to forgive. If you can't learn to demonstrate that now after all our family has been through…I will never to speak to either of you again.

*(**MARIA** exits.)*

ANTHONY. She's good.

(An awkward silence. They both go to the coffin and kneel next to each other.)

PETER. Remember what Daddy said when he found out I was gay?

ANTHONY. No.

PETER. He said, "All I want is a Grandchild." I felt so bad. I felt like disappointed him so much.

ANTHONY. Now Maria will give him one.

PETER. Jonah Horowitz.

(They both chuckle at the thought.)

ANTHONY. At least we don't have to fight about who the Godfather is.

*(**PETER** looks at his Father and starts to cry. He has a very tender moment looking at his Dad. **ANTHONY** stays strong and looks up as if his Father is watching and knows what he has to do. **ANTHONY** slowly puts his hand on his shoulder and consoles him.)*

PETER. I am so sorry that I hurt you.

(**ANTHONY** *finally breaks and puts his hand on his.*)

ANTHONY. We are having the repass at Angelina's.

PETER. Fine. Who's doing the eulogy?

ANTHONY. Who would Daddy want to give his Eulogy?

(*They look to their father.*)

ANTHONY/PETER. Me.

(*They rise.*)

PETER. Will you come to my wedding?

ANTHONY. I'll think about it.

PETER. Will you be my best man?

ANTHONY. *(takes it in for a moment)* No.

(*They start to exit.*)

PETER. Bye Daddy.

ANTHONY. I love you Daddy.

PETER. We were very lucky.

ANTHONY. He may have judged a lot of people...but he never judged us.

(**ANTHONY** *breaks and has a moment. He finally calls his brother into a hug and they embrace.*)

PETER. Are we good?

ANTHONY. We're good!

(*They start to exit then* **ANTHONY** *stops.*)

ANTHONY. Peter, tell them I just need one more minute alone with Daddy.

PETER. Sure. Take your time.

(**ANTHONY** *takes a moment, and then slowly approaches the coffin tentatively like he did in the beginning.*)

ANTHONY. Okay Okay! You got your way! Are you happy now? I made peace with your son. And as always... you were right. It feels good. It feels good to have a brother again. But you had to let everyone know about

Andrew! You just had to let that one out. You never liked him. You always said you have to find a nice Italian boy, you have to find a nice Italian boy…well I never found one! Okay look…I don't know if I believe in all this Vidal nonsense, but somehow I just get this feeling that you were here today. So if you are here… send me a sign. Send me a sign and let me know that you got my back.

(EZIO enters.)

EZIO. Anthony?

ANTHONY. Yes! I'm sorry, I know we have to leave…

EZIO. No, no, take your time. You don't remember me, do you?

ANTHONY. I don't…wait a second…Ezio?

(He nods.)

ANTHONY. The bartender from Spectrum Ezio?

EZIO. Do you know anyone else with that name?

ANTHONY. No, I just didn't recognize you with a shirt on.

EZIO. My work attire has changed.

ANTHONY. What are you doing here?

EZIO. I own the funeral home. When Spectrum closed my Dad was very sick and it was his dying wish that I take it over…so, here I am.

ANTHONY. Oh wow. That's beautiful. You look…great!

EZIO. Thanks, so do you. How is Andrew?

ANTHONY. We recently separated.

EZIO. I'm so sorry to hear that. Was it mutual?

ANTHONY. No, he left me for a twenty-five year old hairdresser named Jose and moved to San Juan. They have a condo on the beach, eighty degree weather every day and a little dog named Poco. I wish them all the happiness in the world.

EZIO. You do?

ANTHONY. Not really.

EZIO. Well I know what you're going through, Lorenzo and I broke up last year.

ANTHONY. Oh, I'm so sorry.

EZIO. It's okay. Single again, what can you do…

ANTHONY. I know what can you do. *(turns away and takes his wedding ring off)*

EZIO. Well, let me know if you need anything. I'll give you my number before you leave and if you ever want to go for coffee or dinner or something…

ANTHONY. I would love that.

*(***EZIO*** politely excuses himself. Once he is gone* ***ANTHONY*** *looks back at his father and then up into the air and blows a kiss up above.)*

Thank you, Daddy!

*(***ANTHONY*** starts to exit and then turns back and looks at his father one more time as the curtain call music begins to fade in….)*

And by the way…you look good!

(Blackout and curtain call music pumps in full.)

(curtain call)